W9-CCN-420

Copyright © 2020 Disney Enterprises, Inc.

All rights reserved. Published by Disney Press, an imprint of Buena Vista Books, Inc. No part of this book may be reproduced or transmitted in any form or by any means, electronic or mechanical, including photocopying, recording, or by any information storage and retrieval system, without written permission from the publisher. For information address Disney Press, 1200 Grand Central Avenue, Glendale, California 91201.

Printed in the United States of America

First Hardcover Edition, July 2020

3 5 7 9 10 8 6 4 2

FAC-034274-20268

Library of Congress Control Number: 2019952658

ISBN 978-1-368-06024-0

Visit disneybooks.com

Disney

The One And Only IVAN

DRAW ME A STORY

Written by BETH FERRY

Drawings by GONZALO KENNY

DISNEY PRESS

Los Angeles • New York

Ivan was a gorilla.

The only gorilla at the Big Top Mall.

The mall was a strange place to find a silverback gorilla, but sometimes the most magnificent things are found in unexpected places.

Murphy

Henrietta

Thelma

The mall was Ivan's home, and he was happy there, mainly because it was filled with his friends. There was Thelma and Murphy and Henrietta. Frankie and Bob.

Frankie

Bob

And then there was

Ruby.

Ruby was the newest member of the Big Top, and she had a *lot* to learn.

"Those are sneakers," Ivan informed her. "Humans think sneakers make them run fast, like cheetahs.

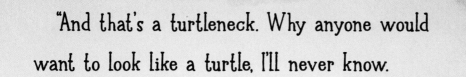

"And that's a turtleneck. Why anyone would want to look like a turtle, I'll never know.

"And that green stuff? Dry leaves. But humans don't eat them. They prefer the pink clouds."

"What's that?"

Ruby asked, pointing at a pile of sticks.

"Crayons," said Ivan.
"They help me *draw* pink clouds . . .
and blue lakes and green forests."

"Ivan is crazy about
his crayons!" Bob piped up.
"And his drawings."

Bob was right.
Ivan's domain was
filled with drawings.

Drawings of
beetles and
bananas.

Drawings of
**beautiful
places**.

Drawings of **old
friends** and
**promises
made**.

by Julia

I L♥ve YOU STeLLa

STELLA

"Draw me!" Bob demanded. "You never draw me. I am completely drawable. And adorable!"

"It doesn't always work like that," Ivan said. "Art has to come from the heart."

"Well, I sleep on your heart every night. Doesn't that count for something?"

"It accounts for my matted fur," Ivan replied.

"Can I try drawing?" Ruby asked.

Ivan handed her a crayon.

Ruby looked closely into Ivan's eye.

Then she drew it.

She studied her own eye.

Then she drew that.
"Look," she said. "Our eyes
are the same."

And they were, both round and dark and beautiful.

Ruby finished drawing Ivan, then rummaged through the pile.

"Where's the color of me?" she asked.

There was no crayon that matched Ruby's wrinkly skin.

Ivan reached for a small box. Inside was a silver
crayon his human friend Julia had given him.

"Silver for
the silverback,"
she had said.

Ivan had been saving it for something important.

"That's not the color of me," Ruby said.
"It's so bright and shiny and special."

Ivan laughed.

"That's exactly
    what you are, Ruby.
        On the inside."

Ruby hesitantly took the crayon.

"Go ahead," Ivan said. "Sometimes art isn't just what you see. Sometimes it's what you feel."

Ruby colored herself silver.

And Ivan was right.

She did look exactly how Ivan made her feel.

She added some more silver to the drawing.

"Silver for the silverback!" she said.

Then she handed him the crayon.

"Will you draw me a story?" Ruby asked.

Ivan wasn't very good at telling stories in words. Maybe he'd be better at telling one in pictures.

He thought for a long time.

Then he drew line after line after line.

And, finally, two lines next to each other.

"Whoa,"

said Bob. "Is that modern art?"

Ivan arranged the pages on the floor.

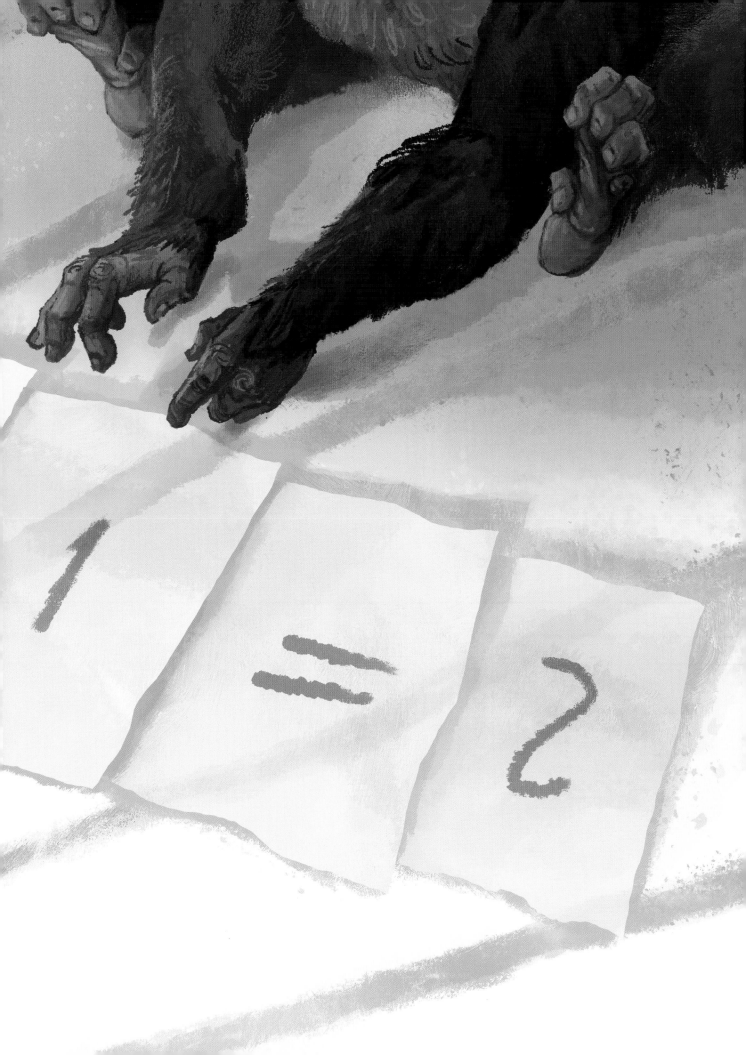

"That's not a story," Bob said. "That's math."

"It *is* a story. It's the story of us," Ivan told Ruby.

"The **One** and Only Ivan
and the **One** and Only Ruby,
always **Two**-gether."

"Bob too?" Ruby asked.

"Bob too!" Ivan agreed.

"And Thelma and Murphy and Frankie
and Henrietta," she added.

"That makes seven," Bob said.

"It makes one," Ruby corrected. "One family."

Ruby was the newest member of the Big Top, and she had a *lot* to learn, but she already knew the most important thing—that her friends were her family.

Did you know the character of Ivan was based on a true story? Ivan was a lowland gorilla born in 1962 in central Africa. He was saved from  poachers in the wild and spent the next twenty-seven years of his life in a concrete enclosure at a shopping mall in Tacoma, Washington. In 1995, the animal rights group PAWS successfully raised thirty thousand dollars to purchase Ivan and relocate him to the Atlanta Zoo, where he spent the rest of his years in peace. His life remains an example of the hope a community can inspire, and the change it can create.